Ring

Contents	Page
School bells	2-3
Stop for trains	4-5
Town clock	6-7
Bells on cats	8-9
Cowbells	10-11
Bells on bikes	12-13
Doorbells	14-15
Phone bells ring	16

written by Pam Holden

Bells ring at school to tell the time.

Bells ring at a crossing when a train is coming.

crossing

They ring to tell people to stop.

Bells ring on a big clock in town.

clock

They ring to tell people the time.

A cat can have a bell on its neck.

It rings to tell birds when a cat is coming.

cat

A cow can have a bell on its neck.

cow

It rings so the farmer can find his cow.

A bike has a bell for the rider to ring.

bike bell

It tells people to get out of the way.

A bell rings at the door of a house.

doorbell

It rings to say that there are visitors.

A bell rings on a phone, too. Hello!